Mouse and Tim

Mouse and Tim

by
Faith McNulty

**Pictures by
Marc Simont**

Harper & Row, Publishers
New York, Hagerstown, San Francisco, London

Mouse and Tim
Text copyright © 1978 by Faith McNulty
Illustrations copyright © 1978 by Marc Simont
All rights reserved. No part of this book may be used or
reproduced in any manner whatsoever without written
permission except in the case of brief quotations embodied
in critical articles and reviews. Printed in the United
States of America. For information address Harper & Row,
Publishers, Inc., 10 East 53rd Street, New York, N.Y. 10022.
Published simultaneously in Canada by Fitzhenry & Whiteside
Limited, Toronto.
First Edition

Library of Congress Cataloging in Publication Data
McNulty, Faith.
    Mouse and Tim.

    SUMMARY: A boy and a mouse describe their relation-
ship during the months they spend together.
      [1. Mice—Fiction.   2. Friendship—Fiction]
I. Simont, Marc. II. Title.
PZ7.M24Mo   [E]   77-11845
ISBN 0-06-024156-X
ISBN 0-06-024157-8 lib bdg.

For Mouse
and Richard who found her.

I am Tim.
This is a picture of Mouse.
She was my mouse.
For a while she lived with me.

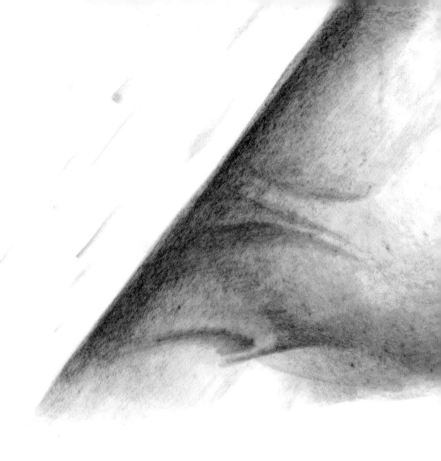

I kept Mouse in a cage
but Mouse was born wild.
She was a deer mouse.
Deer mice live in woods and fields.
Sometimes they live in old barns.
That's where I found Mouse . . .
in our barn.

I was in a nest . . . warm and dark.
I felt my mother's soft fur
and smelled her mouse smell.
Her tongue licked me
while I sucked sweet milk.
Other mouselings pushed against me.
I heard their voices.
I felt their hearts beating
as we lay in a warm heap.

I heard a noise . . . swish . . . swish
getting louder.
My mother was gone.
The nest was gone.
I saw bright cold light. . . .

I felt cold all around me. . . .
I ran, looking for the nest . . .
for the dark . . . for warm fur. . . .
I couldn't run anymore. . . .
I shut my eyes and lay still.

11

On the floor I saw a tiny mouse
no bigger than a bumblebee.
I picked it up.
I thought it was dead.
Its gray fur was finer than velvet.
It had big ears, long whiskers,
and paws like tiny hands.
It was so small and so perfect
I was sorry it was dead.

I felt warmth under me and around me.
I smelled a strange, strong smell.
I felt the ground move and shake.

I held the tiny mouse
inside my two hands
and ran to show Mom and Dad.
I lifted my hand.
Mouse was alive!
Her eyes were open. Her ears trembled.
Dad said, "I swept the barn this morning.
Maybe I swept out a nest of mice with the trash."

I had a gumdrop in my pocket.
I put it beside Mouse.
They were the same size.
She took huge bites. . . .
She ate like a tiger.
I hadn't known such a tiny animal
could be so hungry . . .
and want so much to live.

I smelled a strong, good smell.
I ate sweet, strange stuff
and felt warm inside.

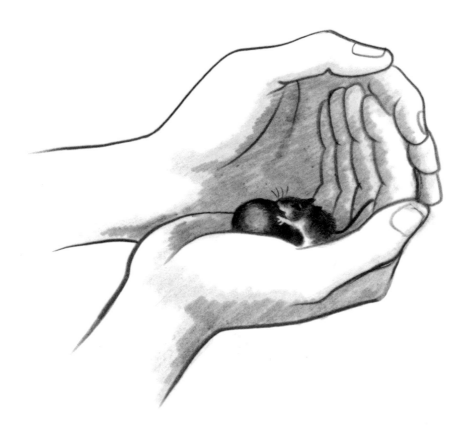

I heard big voices.
I saw big things moving.
Underneath me was a warm hollow. . . .
I crouched.
My heart beat very fast.
I waited.

I said, "Mom, can I keep it?"
Mom said, "For a little while.
Until it is big enough to go back to the wild."
I made Mouse a cage.
In it I put a coconut shell
with a mouse-size door
and scraps of wool for a nest.

I was in a new place.
I ran. I smelled. I tasted.
Everything was strange.
Then I found a hole. . . .
Inside, it was warm and dark and safe.
I went to sleep.

Mouse slept a lot.
Whenever I lifted the coconut shell
I would find her curled up in bed.
When I touched her she would stretch and yawn.
Her whiskers quivered
as she smelled the food I brought.
When I stroked her she closed her eyes.
Sometimes she nibbled my fingers gently . . .
the way mice nibble each other's fur.

I was alone in my nest.
Except when Tim came.
His hands were warm and alive.
He brought delicious food.
I liked his hands.
I nibbled them and felt good.

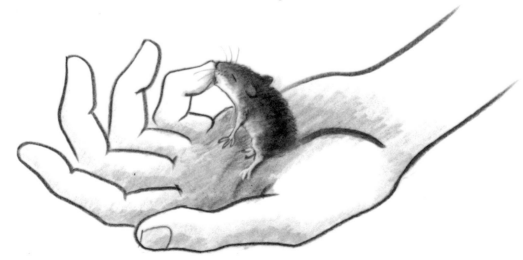

Mouse grew quickly.
In a few weeks she was three times bigger.
She turned reddish brown
with a white belly and white socks.
She washed herself with her tongue like a cat.
She held her tail in her paws and washed that, too.
She was the prettiest mouse you ever saw.

Sometimes Tim's hands and I
went on long trips to new places.

Mouse would jump into my palm
and I would carry her to my bed and let her loose.
She loved to explore.

She ran up my arm.
She sat on my shoulder and nibbled my ear.
She tasted my hair.
She ran down my leg and tugged at my shoelaces.
She was curious about everything in the world.

I climbed mountains
and crept into valleys.
I tasted new tastes and
smelled new smells.

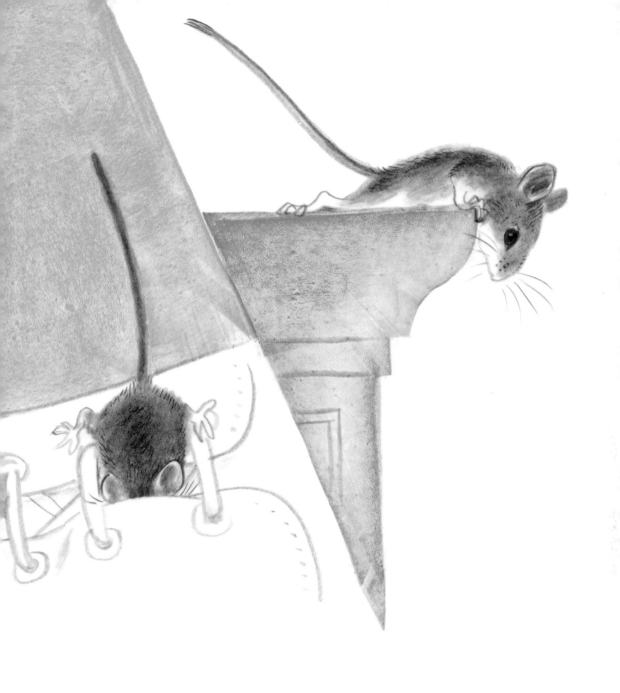

Sometimes I went too far and was afraid.
Then Tim's hands came for me.
I jumped into them and was safe again.

I loved to play with Mouse.
I wondered what she thought of me.
I was so big
she couldn't see me all at once,
but I felt she *knew* me.
When I held her in my hand
a feeling seemed to pass between us.
Mouse was very smart.
I wondered how she could think so well
with such a tiny brain.
Then I thought: Our clock is a foot high.
Mother's watch is the size of a nickel,
but they both tell time.
I thought of how Mouse and I
saw the same things in different ways.
Once I put her on the kitchen table. . . .

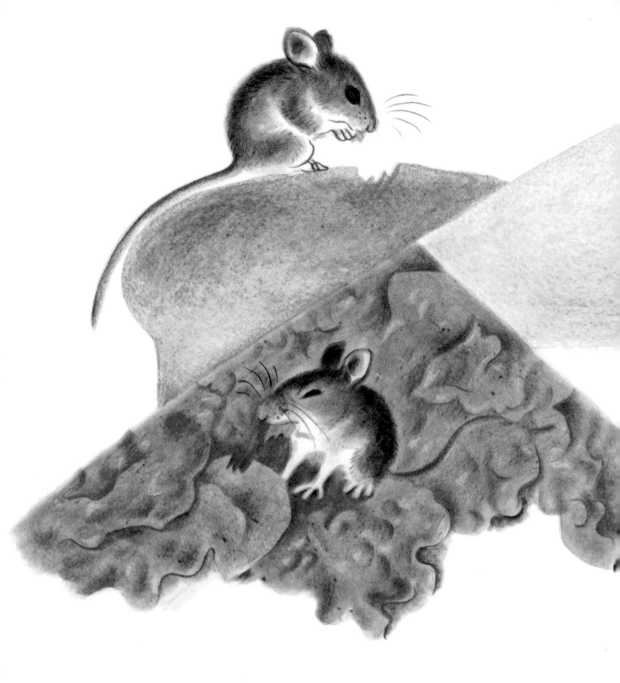

I climbed up a delicious mountain
and took a bite. . . .
I ran into a deep forest. . . . It was bitter. . . .
I ran out and found a huge, sweet-smelling thing.
I tried to taste it, but it ran away. . . .

Mouse tried to bite into an apple.
It was too big. It rolled away.
I thought: Mouse and I live
in different worlds at the same time.

Mice like to run.
I made a wheel for Mouse
and put it in her cage.
It turned as she ran.
I kept her cage by my bed.
Sometimes at night I woke
and heard the wheel creak
as Mouse ran and ran and ran.

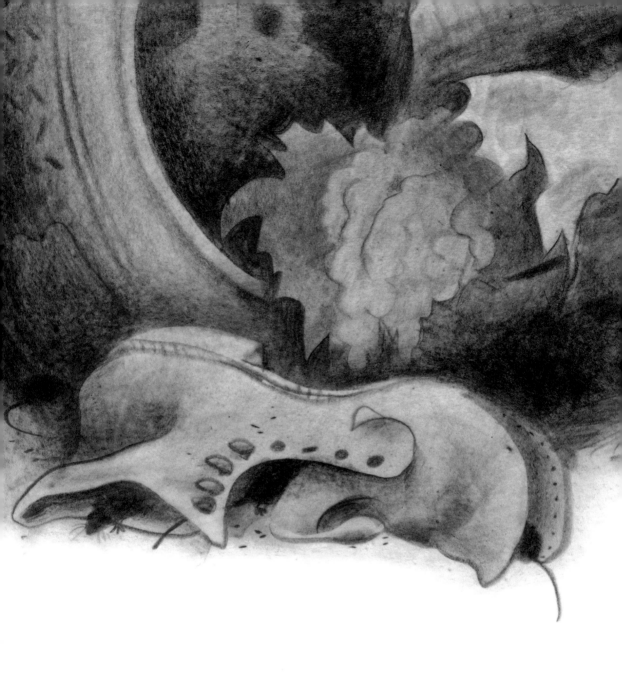

Asleep in my house I dreamed.
I dreamed of running through tunnels.
I dreamed of smells—
food smells, fur smells, mouse smells.

I dreamed of sounds—
rustling, whispering, squeaking.
I dreamed of mouse voices I heard long ago.
Then I would wake up
and run and run and run.

One night I woke. It was moonlight.
I saw Mouse sitting up.
I saw her eyes shine . . . her ears quiver. . . .
What did she see and hear and smell?

I saw silver light.
I saw shadows move. I heard Tim breathing.
A moth fluttering . . . I smelled night air.
Then I smelled a different smell . . . a mouse . . .
coming closer and closer.
Tim's bed creaked.
Mouse feet ran away.
I began to run, too.
I ran and ran, but found nothing.

When Mouse ran on her wheel,
where was she trying to go?

I found Mouse in April.
Now it was August.
Mom said, "Mouse is grown up.
It is time to let her go."
I said, "She's my mouse.
I want to keep her."
Mom said, "Would you want
to spend your life in a cage?"

It was warm.
The night air was sweet.
Tim brought new food.
I ate clover and blueberries.
He brought roots and I smelled the earth.
He brought moths.
I caught them fluttering and ate them.

I taught Mouse to eat wild food.
I knew that soon I must let her go.

The day came.
At sunset I took Mouse to the barn.
I sat on a woodpile
and held her in my hand.
I stroked her.
With my fingertips I told her
that I loved her—that I hoped she
would be safe out in the world.

I was in Tim's hand.
I smelled dust and hay
and old wood.
I nibbled on his hand.

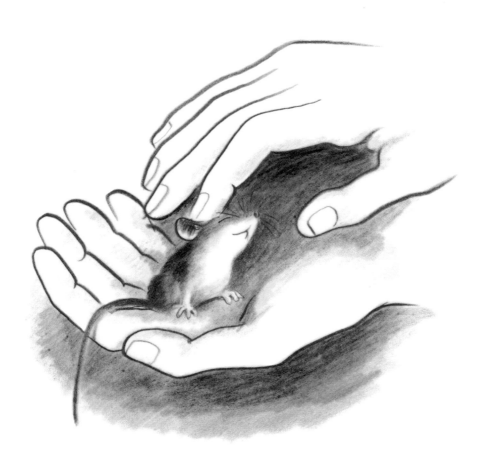

I put Mouse on the woodpile.
She ran into a dark nook. . . .
I didn't want to leave.
I sat in the twilight
and wondered what she was doing.
Was she happy to be free?

I ran. I was dizzy with new smells, new paths. . . .
I was lost. I was afraid.
I followed the smell of my footprints back to Tim.
I waited beside him.
I waited for him to put out his hand.

I stayed until the moon rose.
There was no sign of Mouse.
It was time to go.
I said, "Good-bye, Mousie. Good luck.
I'll miss you, little mouse," and I went away.

Tim turned into a huge black shadow.
He disappeared.
I didn't know which way to go.
There were so many strange tunnels and paths.
Then I heard a voice—small and faraway—
a voice like mine.
I ran toward it in the sweet-smelling dark.

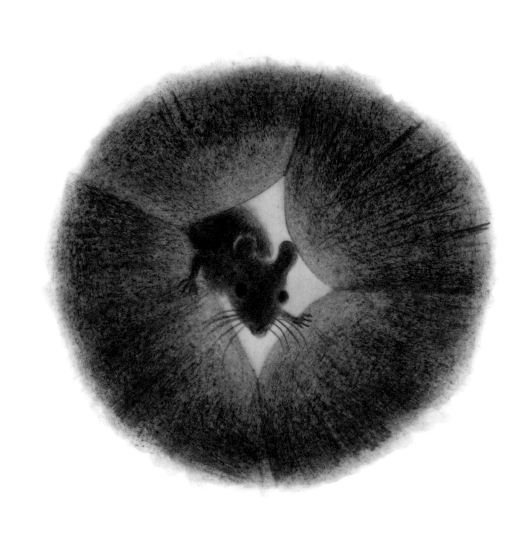